Mimi Braun Remembers

Mimi Braun Remembers

Miriam Braun

Rutledge Books, Inc.

Danbury, CT

Interior design by Kelly Rothen

Rutledge Books, Inc.
107 Mill Plain Road, Danbury, CT 06811
1-800-278-8533
www.rutledgebooks.com

Manufactured in the United States of America

Cataloging in Publication Data
Schwartz, Jane K.

Mimi Braun Remembers

ISBN: 1-58244-160-X

1. Memoir -- Mimi Braun. 2. Successful Marriage.
3. Spiritual transcendence. 4. Civic responsibility.

Library of Congress Control Number: 2001090787

Table of Contents

June 1993

Letter to

Her Husband

Letter to

Her Husband

Darling Siggy,

It is nearly four and a half years since you died. I am so tired of waiting to join you. I talk to you almost every minute of every day and can't help but feel you are listening in some way. My deepest hope, the one thing that keeps me going, is that you are—and that you, too, are waiting before you go on to some final form of consciousness with me.

During these years since you left, I have been telling myself that I would put on paper the events of my life with you. Why does that thought offer some comfort and surcease from the terrible loneliness I never knew was possible before I lost you? I don't know, but I've determined to try it, since no other activity has brought relief.

And honey, I have been active, as you know if you are watching. I mastered, to a degree (not in your class, of course), the management of our finances. My fervent thanks that you left me well off. As we used to say, "Maybe money can't make you happy, but it can keep you mighty comfortable while you're being miserable." That's no joke; it's exactly my situation. I haven't stinted myself, but I've given away more money than I've spent. I approve of that, especially the physics fellowship in your name, but it brings me no joy. Your life and works deserve far more celebration than that, but at least that much, with the help of your wonderfully enthusiastic colleagues and the

university, has been done. Despite the intensity of my grief and loneliness, I have managed to keep my self-respect intact in that connection and others. I haven't troubled our children with any woe, not of
feeling or of physical ailment or demands on time and attention. I
entertain friends at home and out and am invited out quite a bit. I do
my volunteer tutoring. I keep the house and garden in pretty good
shape. They are still my favorite places, which is why I can't move to
some retirement community or another house closer to town.

But honey, it is so lonely—lonely not just at home, but in the
midst of friends, lonely traveling, sightseeing, shopping. All the good
people I see don't reach me. I need the voice of love to speak to me.
That was you, and now it is no more; not just love, but intelligence,
knowledge, wisdom, responsiveness. In all the years, there were
never a mind and heart like yours. I was lucky enough to live with
that for fifty-two years. I can't get used to living without it, but I can't
go either. I must endure this purgatory, hoping it has a purpose
beyond my ken, that perhaps I won't have to die before the knot of
pain constantly in the center of me will vanish and I will know, if not
joy, at least the equanimity I mostly used to live with.

Writing is very hard. When I look back I have never said it right,
despite many changes and corrections. Still, I will learn to use this
electric typewriter (no chance that at eighty I will buy and learn to
use a word processor), and see what comes of it.

College
College

College

Miriam Feinstein shed the "Miriam" on entering college and became "Mimi" to everyone. She met Sigmund Braun when he was a graduate student and she a sophomore. He was an occasional ornament around the sorority house when he came to pick up the soror, Elly, who was his girlfriend. He wasn't handsome or tall, and he limped from the residue of polio. In the spring, in a T-shirt, however, he looked like the famous Charles Atlas ads, muscles bulging, thick neck, a magnificent physical specimen. His smile, his voice, his casual conversation, seemed to charm the girls he talked to, although Mimi herself never joined in any group around him. She admired him in a remote kind of way. Mimi didn't even know then that he had two teaching assistantships, one in physics, one in gymnastics.

Mimi was starting her own love affair that spring. She was agreeing to become lovers with David, although they had no place in which to make love because David had no car and no apartment. The garden behind the sorority house, fragrant with wisteria, was where they "plighted their troth." She was eighteen and he twenty-one, both virgins, both trembling with desire as he kissed her breasts, an experience new and overwhelming. He was about to graduate, but he had a teaching fellowship in European history for the next two years and had arranged for a private apartment with a separate entrance, in the home of a professor. In the fall, they would begin a complete love life.

David was a poor boy from the Bronx, not handsome or athletic, but nice-enough looking. His exceptional intelligence and scholarly ways won him scholarships to pay for four years of college at a time when these were awarded on a competitive basis solely with no consideration for financial need. He was the most articulate man Mimi had ever met. She found him endlessly charming, witty, and knowledgeable, while the intensity of his desire stirred her deeply. She decided he was the lover she had been waiting for. The attraction was of a different order of magnitude from her feelings for the youths with whom she had exchanged kisses before.

In the fall, Sigmund Braun disappeared from view, having at age twenty-three taken himself off with a Ph.D. into the working world. The love affair with David ushered Mimi into a new world of pleasure and relief from the anxieties and depression that had plagued her throughout her adolescence. She felt delivered from the search for love that had begun at age thirteen, the terrible aching longing that no prior suitor or date, of whom there had been several, including proposals of marriage, had been able to free her.

Mimi had known all her life that she was a moderately pretty girl and a good student but felt a lack of special talents as well as a timidity which deterred her from undertaking many activities. Many girls seemed more accomplished and self-confident. Yet at one point in her junior year a soror told her she was the best-liked girl in the house and that everybody agreed she had the best figure. The considerable self-confidence which arose from this disclosure stayed with Mimi for the rest of her life, but she took little pride in it. It was easy to like people, be sensitive to their feelings, and be liked in return. Achievement—particularly intellectual achievement—was what she admired most in others and desired for herself.

In later years, Mimi realized that she had been a prototype of Jewish youth at that time, the child of shtetl Jews who revered learning. Two sisters, ten and twelve years Mimi's senior, had been the only graduates of their small-town high school who had gone on to

college. Mimi's father, the immigrant owner of the town's only clothing store, had been a "yeshiva bocher" who continued his Hebrew
reading on his own throughout his life. College was a serious business; a career was required. Both sisters were schoolteachers. Mimi
majored in psychology with a minor in biology and took education
courses that would enable her to teach if, by some miracle, a teaching
job became available when she graduated in the deep depression of
1933. She didn't want to teach, however.

In the middle of her senior year, David developed cold feet. He
had secured a fellowship to study in Paris the next year. Who knew
when and if he could marry her? He thought it was wrong to keep
her from seeing other men and jeopardizing her chances for marriage. Marriage had not been in her mind. She had expected the love
affair to lapse with graduation and was more disheartened than
heartbroken. She did not want to abandon the warmth and security
of this love and go looking for others. Only a week went by before
David was back on the phone wanting to see her. They would each
feel free to date others but would continue to see each other. She
agreed. He exercised his freedom by taking out one of her sorority sisters. At this point, Mimi realized that David's charming egotism
included a remarkable insensitivity to her feelings and that he could
not be counted on to cherish her at all. She essentially gave up any
expectation of a future with him. She accepted invitations from a couple of attractive men she knew but felt lost and betrayed.

During Mimi's junior year, she and a sorority sister, Helen, drove
with a friend to R_____ to visit Mimi's sister, Rachel.

"You know who's living in R_____ ?" asked Helen. "Siggy
Braun. He just got a good job there. We keep in touch now and then.
You know, he's wonderful. I never could have passed freshman
physics without his help. Let's call him."

So it was that Siggy Braun was invited to visit and get to know
Mimi's sister, Rachel, and her husband. He was working as a research
physicist with a large corporation. He greeted them enthusiastically,

and Mimi noted up close how pleasantly expressive were his large, light-brown eyes, his voice, and the content of his speech. He told them that he frequently drove to New York to see Elly and also his parents.

The next time Mimi visited her sister from school, she called Siggy, and they kept in touch with an occasional note as well.

Luckily for Mimi, the chairman of the psychology department, with whom she took courses and had frequent conferences, considered her a superior student. Still, in the spring of her senior year he could offer her no graduate fellowship. There was no money to pay for graduate work on her own, but he found her a training job in a psychological clinic attached to a state mental hospital. It would pay no salary but would provide room and board. Not one of her friends had a job waiting after graduation, and Mimi could hardly believe her luck. The job would start in September and, acting on advice from her professor, she would take a special summer course in psychological testing in R_____, living with her sister. Mimi knew very well that she was not in a class with David and Siggy when it came to brains and scholarship, but she believed she could do well professionally, with graduate school in view if money somehow became available. She left school with her parents, therefore, feeling sad and yet hopeful. Saying good-bye to David was a wrench, especially because of her inner certainty that this was a permanent parting. He promised to write from Paris and to see her as soon as he could come home for a visit.

On Her Own

On Her Own

On Her Own

The summer courses went well, but afterward, at home with her parents, Mimi helped take care of her single sister, Molly, who was recuperating from plastic surgery for nose reconstruction and suffering an emotional collapse. Molly had for years considered herself ugly because of a large and somewhat misshapen nose, the latter the result of a bicycling accident. Mimi, since she was eight or nine, had suffered with Molly's unhappiness and datelessness with men. She approved of Molly's undertaking the "nose job" but was shocked by the trauma it caused. Molly wept because her face was transformed by the not-yet-healed surgery. Their mother tried to comfort; poor, kind, loving Mother, sensible and capable, but quite out of tune with the American milieu of college and city life to which her daughters had emigrated, even as she had emigrated from a Russian-Polish ghetto to small-town America. Heartache, heartache.

Thus Mimi left for her new job oppressed by considerable anxiety. She was wonderfully well received, however, by the chief psychologist and two other psychological interns, girls just out of college like herself. The three young women shared two rooms, comfortable and well furnished, in a wing of the grim old main hospital building and ate in the employees' cafeteria. Their quarters had a private entrance, but one wall adjoined a hospital corridor where patients were housed.

On one of her first nights, Mimi was awakened by a wailing on the other side of the wall. It heightened to a crescendo, faded, then returned, as if the person were walking back and forth along a corridor, weeping continuously. Mimi's heart leapt. Although the sound finally stopped, she couldn't get back to sleep. She didn't want to awaken her roommates, but in the morning asked about it. Yes, they said, it was undoubtedly a patient wailing in the night. They had heard it a time or two before her arrival. Didn't it bother them? No, not really, because patients were expected to be troubled; it was part of the environment.

As the weeks went by, Mimi had more and more difficulty sleeping, waiting with baited breath for the terrible sound to start, which it did from time to time. Fear began to oppress her though the days as well. With it came the thought: I could become like these poor patients. There are so many of them. How common this mental illness is. Then her fear would leap and overwhelm her. Finally she talked to the chief psychologist about the problem. He suggested that she see one of the staff psychiatrists. She made an appointment to do so.

After describing to the psychiatrist what was happening to her and something about her previous life, including the affair with David, the woman told her that she was suffering from a sexual abstinence neurosis and should seek treatment. At that point, all Mimi's fears were confirmed: She was indeed like one of the patients. Terror consumed her.

Mimi had met her parents in New York a few weeks before, and her mother, to whom she confided nothing, had commented on her apparently trembling demeanor and asked about the job. Mimi had been noncommittal, but her mother, who rarely gave advice, suggested that Mimi should consider leaving.

Now, from the depths of Mimi's being came a command: You must get away from this place!

She went home, jobless, to the familiar environment. Fear came and went, also shame and depression over the ruin of her career.

Through all of this, Mimi had one tremendously helpful confidant—Siggy Braun. He had written to her at the hospital, and she had found herself able to describe to him, in a letter, what was happening to her. He replied with utmost reassurance: her reaction was perfectly understandable, and there was no reason in the world why she should fear for her sanity. Every medical student, he told her, studying various diseases in depth for the first time, was certain that he was contracting most of them.

It was decided that Mimi would go live with her sister and look for a job in R_____. First, she went to the university to see her professor, to explain and apologize for her defection. This worried her greatly, but she knew she must repay his kindness with at least this much. She told him the story and how badly she felt about betraying his faith in her. He was very understanding. That was the last contact she ever had with him.

The first person she called upon arriving at her sister's was Siggy Braun. He came over immediately.

"Oh Siggy, it's so wonderful to see you. Thank you, thank you for your understanding—you saved my life. You really are wonderful, you know, just like Helen used to say."

"Are you okay? You look fine, beautiful in fact, but are you really feeling better?"

"Yes—kind of shaky, maybe, and terribly disappointed, but the acute stage seems to have passed."

"Come on out with me, we'll go somewhere and talk."

He drove her to an elegant roadhouse, a speakeasy on the outskirts of town. Prohibition repeal was still some months away, and this was the kind of place popular and well known around cities at the time but outside Mimi's experience. One large room housed a handsome bar and small tables, the other a dining room and dance floor with a jazz band. Upstairs, Siggy told her, there was reputed to be gambling, although he hadn't tried it. Mimi was enchanted. The closest she had ever come to high living and drinking was fraternity house parties with their terrible-tasting bootleg hooch, and she hadn't gone to many of those because her last two years at school had been spent frugally with David.

Siggy, easily at home in this environment, let the headwaiter lead them to a small table in the bar and present them with a list of drinks.

"What would you like to drink?" asked Siggy.

"I don't know. I've never seen such a list or a place like this."

"Let's see—something that tastes good, probably."

He turned to the waiter. "Let's have one sidecar and an old-fashioned."

"The old-fashioned for me, I guess," said Mimi.

"Just the opposite," Siggy laughed. "I get the old-fashioned and you get the tough-sounding sidecar."

The sidecar was absolutely delicious, seemingly without alcohol, and it quickly expanded her sense of well-being.

"How do you know about these drinks?" asked Mimi, whose own exposure to alcohol was limited to the sacramental sweet wine made by her mother or the mule-kick of bootleg whisky.

"My family, especially my mother and aunts, grew up with civilized living and tried not to let Prohibition interfere."

Siggy's father was a physician, and two of his aunts owned a successful custom women's wear business with summer trips to Paris in the '20s to look at fashion collections. "At least it was successful until the last couple of depression years," he said.

They talked effortlessly about many things as Mimi was enveloped in a rosy glow. For the first time since school last spring, her pervasive anxiety disappeared. It was not just the place and the drink, but also that she felt she had never known such sympathetic responsiveness from any other person. He was still driving to New York on some weekends to see his parents and Elly. He still hoped to marry Elly if she would only make up her mind. She was teaching part time in a dance studio for children, looking for work, and worrying about being dependent on her mother and stepfather.

"Not that they can't afford it," said Siggy. "In spite of the depression, he's a big developer and really rich. Still, it's wonderful to be self-supporting and independent. These past couple of years have been great for me. I'm glad I went into industry instead of teaching, as I'd been tempted to do. I like teaching, but my research is fascinating and it also pays well by today's standards."

From that night on, she saw Siggy every week or two, and usually they went for a drink to one speakeasy or another. These were her happy times. Her job search was not fruitful. The few clinics in town that did psychological testing had no place for her, and even full-time department store sales jobs or office clerical and typing work were unavailable. She was hired by one department store for some Saturday and special sales but could get nothing regular. Selling depressed her, but she was glad for the few dollars it gave her for personal needs. Luckily, her sister, whose teaching provided a secure income, and the latter's husband, Ben, whose small wholesale business did not, were both indulgent about keeping her while she marked time.

Shortly after her arrival at R_____ she learned from a soror with whom she corresponded that a classmate, Sol Rosen, with whom she had spent an evening during senior week, was in medical school at the University of R_____. He sounded lonely, said her friend, and gave Mimi his address and phone number. Mimi decided to call him and was overwhelmed.

"Oh," he exclaimed, "I'm so glad to hear from you! You have no idea how impossible life is here. What are you doing in this terrible town?"

She told him.

"Look, this very night I'm supposed to go to a boring party with a lot of tiresome people. If you could come with me you could save my life."

She was astonished but game. He had no car, but friends would drive him to pick her up. The party was at somebody's house, perhaps a dozen college-age or recent graduates were there, and in the background were parents who exercised no restraint on the considerable alcohol consumed. Mimi drank enough to get tipsy early in order to lose her self-consciousness and spent the evening amazed by the effervescent Sol, who appeared to enchant everybody. All remarks, all responses, seemed to be addressed to him. He drank a lot but stayed coherent in an odd kind of way, with often convoluted, unfinished sentences, quotations, and compliments. Although he was in medical school, his conversation carried no reference to class work.

Mimi was surprised when he called her the next day, Sunday, because she felt she had pretty much melted into the background the night before. Could he come over, perhaps they could go for a walk and a movie? He came by bus and on foot in the bright March afternoon. They sat in the living room briefly, with Rachel, who did not have to ask the loquacious Sol about his activities, interests, and reactions.

"I don't know why I'm here studying medicine," he told her. "Why not—it's considered appropriate," he waved his arms and smiled, looking about the living room. "This is a very attractive room. You should see the place I'm living in—a Victorian mansion, relic of glory days turned boardinghouse. Two charming ladies—really they are—run it for an assortment of characters. I used to live in a fraternity house at college and this is really much better, in its way, which I won't try to describe except to say that it's cheap, the food is okay, and I have a big attic room all to myself and the first privacy of my life. You'll have to come see for yourself."

Would Mimi go for a walk with him? She bundled up, and as they left the house he told her:

"Your sister's very nice, sympathetic—you are, too, you know."

Everything Sol said seemed to come spontaneously, without forethought, and she found herself reacting with a similar spontaneity, as if she were talking to a bright child whose curiosity and opinions bubbled out.

The day was a true foretaste of spring, with chill gone from the air despite vestiges of dirty snow still lingering. To walk leisurely through it was both invigorating and warming. They found a small park, leafless and deserted, and sat on a bench in a little grove of evergreen shrubs. Without intending to, Mimi told him about the hospital experience, omitting reference to the psychiatrist's diagnosis. He was indignant.

"Of course, you were just right. *O de profanum vulgus*—people are such clods—not to be frightened and hurt by all those locked up souls."

"I was working as part of a research program, you know—looking for causes and possible cures for schizophrenia, physiological peculiarities."

"Yes, of course. Very humane. Poor abandoned souls, all the same."

"Listen," Sol said, as they rose and began to walk again. "Tonight there's another party. I wasn't going to go, but I will if you'll go with me."

She went with him, and from then on she saw him about once a week, usually at similar parties at the homes of friends who provided food, drink, and transportation. She drank a lot, along with Sol, who became increasingly euphoric as the evening wore on, as did Mimi in a quieter way.

"You know, Mimi," her sister said one day, "Sol is one of the handsomest men I've ever seen."

"You think so?" Mimi was surprised. She hadn't thought of Sol in those terms. His wildly effervescent personality almost seemed to extinguish his physical self. Most tall, handsome men acted quietly aware of their own presence and exhibited no need to exert charm or individuality. Furthermore, she had started dating a handsome blond young man of Swedish extraction; him, of the light blue eyes and white-blond hair, she considered handsome indeed—so much so that just looking at him aroused a need to fondle, as one might a beautiful blond doll. Having gone out almost exclusively with Jewish youths, she had never expected attentions from someone who looked like the golden knights of Arthurian legends. She was enthralled with him, hardly believing that he found her attractive. He was sweet, too, and intelligent, a recent graduate of an Ivy League college, with a real job as an area sales representative for a national cereal company. The endless kisses they exchanged in his small van never led him to seek more. In truth, he asked her if she thought they might marry. She didn't consider it seriously for a moment; she was incapable of confronting her orthodox parents with such a choice.

"Ah no," she told him. "I do love you, but there's no way that could work."

That was the spring of her blooming as a popular belle, something she had never been. For one Saturday night, seven different young men asked for a date. Incredible, she told herself. She had never understood why some girls attracted many men, and she had certainly never been one of them. She was not flirtatious, although she had often wished she had the capacity. In any case, the flurry of activity submerged her deep disappointment with herself over the panicky flight from the hospital, the current joblessness, and the stalemate of a career.

As a result of her sister's remark, Mimi became aware that Sol was indeed very good to look at—tall and well built, with curly dark hair and narrow, greenish eyes. He did not flirt with girls at parties nor they with him, despite the good looks and effervescence—or perhaps because of the latter. Although Mimi quoted to herself, "A most intense young man, a soulful eyed young man, an ultrapoetical, superaesthetical out of the way young man," unlike Bunthorne, he was neither an aesthete nor a poet. The intensity was surely there, but its focus was mysterious to her. Nor did "Damozels by the score, all weeping and burning, all sighing and yearning, all follow him as before." He was unfathomable, unique.

One Sunday afternoon she and Sol sat by themselves in her

sister's living room listening to a concert on the radio. An orchestra was playing a Cesar Franck symphony that Mimi had never heard. The music was extraordinarily beautiful, and, as occasionally happened with things too beautiful to bear, tears slowly rolled down her cheeks. When the music stopped, she turned to Sol beside her on the sofa to comment on it.

"Why Mimi, what is it, what's the matter?" he exclaimed.

Suddenly aware of the tears, embarrassed, she brushed them away with the back of her hand.

"Oh, nothing. This happens to me sometimes. The music was so exquisite. I'm sorry."

"Thank heaven, I was scared. I thought you were really upset about something."

"Ah Sol, you're so sweet. I love you."

The words had formed themselves without intent, as nearly always happened with him.

"I love you, too!" He put his arms around her and they exchanged a long and passionate kiss. Amazing! For the many nights he had left her at her door, a good-night peck had constituted their farewells.

From that day on they became almost inseparable: a phone call every day or evening, walks in the park through the soft May days, parties many evenings, and kisses, kisses, caresses—in the backseats of friends' cars, in the gardens of host families, on the sofa of her sister's house. Unique kisses, because it was not the delight of desire which predominated, as had previously happened, but an intense awareness of Sol as a rare individual.

Sol had one particular friend, Bert, a bright and very articulate small man, somewhat older, who was starting a business of his own. He seemed to dote on Sol, and it was he who usually drove them around to parties. One evening they met in Sol's room, along with a couple of other friends, for drinks before going on to another party. En route, with Sol and Mimi squeezed in front with Bert, Sol started a monologue with unfamiliar content.

"Ah, woe is me for the wretched blindness of my soul. Which way shall I go? I could become an actor—a rabbi—a doctor—an ascetic..." His voice drifted away. "This mysterious universe sends signals hard to interpret, and yet some are wonderfully clear and commanding. Through the ages men have heard and acted on them. The voice of the creator speaks, not really in words, but in overpowering assurance of—of meaning—of love..."

The monologue went on in this vein for some time, with references to prophets and philosophers. Suddenly Sol exclaimed, "Do you have any idea what I'm talking about?"

Mimi, also quite drunk, answered, "Yes, I do. I don't really think about this, I've never spoken to anyone about it, but a few months ago I had the most extraordinary experience—it shook me—I can't tell you how much. I was at the dentist's. He gave me nitrous oxide for some dental surgery. That happened once before, and when I awoke I told the dentist, 'I just had the funniest dream!'

"'That's what *you* think,' he said, and I realized he was being quizzical because I'd had laughing gas, of course—though I'd never realized it was literally true. I forgot that dream, but this second time the dream was—God—or some equivalent—who filled me with unspeakable ecstasy, something I had never felt before. I was assured beyond a doubt that I was cared for, that I was fundamental to the universe. When I woke, I heard myself saying, 'Wait 'til I tell my sister!'

"'What have you done now, bad girl?' asked the dentist, 'that you have to tell your sister about?'

"What I wanted to tell my sister, Molly, was that the atheism, or agnosticism, which had permeated our lives with the abandonment of our parents' orthodoxy (along with her feelings of worthlessness) was false. God was real and cared for us. Afterward I never told her or anyone else about it. It was still utterly mysterious, quite outside any thought or wish I'd ever had. I kept trying to recapture the feel of it but couldn't."

"Then you *do* know what I mean!" exclaimed Sol.

"You two have been talking the damnedest rot I ever heard in my whole life!" exploded Bert.

Poor Bert, thought Mimi, poor benighted Bert, poor lost soul untouched by the magnificence of creation and his own relation to it.

The ecstasy of the dream under gas returned to her. She and Sol were quite drunk, and exactly what they said to each other throughout the party she never quite remembered. They clung and kissed in a hallway. She was suffused with the certainty of the actual presence of deity who was filling both herself and Sol, then and there, with revelation. In her mind she spoke to the deity: How incredible this is, what a wonderful sense of humor you have, to visit this magnificence on me who never believed you existed! An answer came back: My ways are not yours. Be satisfied.

"Sol, do you have a piece of paper and pen on you? While this is happening I want to write it down so we will never doubt it." He gave her a slip of paper and a pen. She wrote some words, then tucked the paper in the breast pocket of his jacket.

The next morning, after a few hours of sleep, Siggy was on the phone for her.

"Honey, this is spring weekend back at school. I thought I might drive up if you would go with me."

Waking slowly into a heavenly world, she told him, "Oh, that's too bad. I have a date with Sol."

"Well, maybe he'd like to come, too. Why don't you ask him? I haven't been back in a couple of years. We can get around to the fraternity parties, sleep in one or another for a few hours, and drive back tomorrow afternoon. How does that sound?"

"Wonderful! I'll call Sol."

It was arranged, and by early afternoon they were off in Siggy's shiny new V-8 Ford, the three of them in the front seat. Siggy drove fast, 80 miles an hour and more. He also made conversation, mostly with Sol, while Mimi floated in an unknown world. At one point she thought that maybe last night was just a preamble to an immediate exit from this existence into the next via a car smash-up—and felt strangely exhilarated by the prospect.

Before the trip ended, she asked Sol, "Do you have a slip of paper in your jacket pocket?"

He silently pulled it out and handed it to her. She read to herself: "We have said there is a God who knows and cares what we are doing."

The words came as a shock. Such an ordinary thing! What all the world's religions were about, all the belief in a personal deity she had long ago rejected—since her late childhood. She handed the slip back to Sol. He read it, nodded, and wordlessly put it back in his pocket.

From campus party to party they wandered that night, she and Sol always together, Siggy sometimes with them, sometimes off with others. They got drunk, but the unearthly ecstasy that stayed with Mimi was nothing like ordinary alcoholic euphoria. About 5 A.M., she and Sol lay pressed together on a fraternity house sofa, fully clothed, not really making love, and yet the waves of physical desire that swept through her were beyond anything she had ever experienced. On and off they slept, one being.

At one point during the evening Siggy had said to her, "Honey, this is really it, isn't it? You're in love with him, aren't you?"

"Yes, oh yes—," she breathed.

"I'd thought for this little while it might be you and me."

"Oh, Siggy, do you mind? I'm so overwhelmed. Perhaps we shouldn't have come."

"Of course I don't, honey." But there was a certain sad loneliness there, and she felt a fleeting regret, although Siggy had obviously been having a wonderful time, greeted right and left by enthusiastic old friends, colleagues, and students. For eight years he had been a kind of campus celebrity.

If she and Sol had been inseparable before, now they became like one person—an unknown person, outside any prior experience, living in a paradise whose existence she had never dreamed of. It was filled with lighthearted humor, not wit, not the satire she had known with David, not the informed and interesting comment on all phases of life supplied by Siggy, but an all-pervading joy in which the conflict and suffering of the world were absorbed.

One early June evening, sitting in a garden, Sol told her, "I just wrote my father that I want to stay here this summer and take a couple of very good courses. I won't go to the camp counseling job I've had these past years. I'm very excited about it—and you and I can have the summer together."

"How wonderful!"

In each other's arms, no impetus came from either to complete a physical intimacy.

She herself had good news. The psychologist at a child welfare agency had hired her as an assistant, paying a tiny stipend, but she would be training again. The practical aspects of life work themselves out, too.

A week later, however, Sol was in distress. His father had written that it was necessary for him to go to camp and earn some money.

"I hate that place! I don't want to go, I don't want to go!"

Mimi was disappointed, but told him, "It's only for a couple of months. If the money is needed, that's most important. The coming year we'll be together again."

She didn't ask for any details about the camp or why it was so distasteful to him. She felt that he, like herself, could live, in the new spirit that pervaded her, through any difficulties.

The night before he was to leave there was a problem about her seeing him. Her parents had come to town unexpectedly; there was a family dinner, and she hadn't known whether she could get away for the evening with Sol.

She did, however, and in the garden of the house where a usual party took place, he exclaimed, "If you hadn't come tonight, I think I would have gone mad. I love you, I love you, I can't bear to leave this life with you for that miserable job."

Again she comforted him, enthralled with the assurance that the temporary separation would not really hurt.

Through July and August the world of wonder she had entered stayed with her. She wrote to him often—about her new job, the people she knew, and various activities. In July he answered with a couple of short notes, no details of his life—"I hate it up here." In August only one note came before the last one, which gave the early September date when he would return.

On that day, a Saturday, she waited with total expectancy for his call. It did not come until early evening.

"Oh Sol, oh Sol, you're really back. I've been waiting all day for this. I though you were going to arrive earlier."

"I've been back for a couple of hours, but I had to get settled in and tend to some things." His voice didn't echo her delight.

"Can you come over now?"

He did, and they went for a walk in the warm, soft twilight. Her joy bubbled over in an exuberant monologue for a while until she realized he was responding with monosyllables. Her heart began to sink. He was quite unlike himself.

"I know you didn't enjoy it up there, but how are you now? Are you okay?"

"I don't know. I'm tired."

It was not her Sol. Just as his spontaneity had always engendered her own, now she was silenced by his silence. A kind of terror started to rise within her, and she could not express herself to him.

At last he said, "I think I'd better get back. I'll call you tomorrow."

He left her at the door with a light kiss. Many, many years later, reviewing that evening in her mind, she saw the lack of good sense and self-confidence in caring for another person epitomized in her response at the time.

No one was in the house. She threw herself on the bed and gave herself up to an agonizing paroxysm of grief that rose from the depths of her being. When the phone near her bedroom door rang, however, she picked it up—suddenly hoping—but could not control the crack of her voice when she said hello.

"Honey, what is it?" It was Siggy. She couldn't speak.

"Honey, what's the matter? What is it?"

After a pause, "I'm sorry— I'm sorry—it's okay— I'm sorry," she sobbed.

"Honey, I'm coming over right now."

"No, no, it's nothing you can do anything about. I'm okay." Her sobs continued.

"I'll be right there."

He took her in his car to a nearby park. With difficulty, haltingly, she tried to describe the reunion with Sol.

"Why honey, you are overreacting unbelievably. Of course he's tired—had a bad summer, needs to prepare for a new semester at school—has nothing to do with his feelings for you. You are being very silly." So he reassured her over and over again, hugged her, kissed her, and took her home considerably comforted.

The next day Sol did not call, however, and toward evening she called him. He couldn't see her that evening; he was settling into a different room at the boardinghouse. They made a date for the next late afternoon, Monday, when they would walk and meet halfway between his place and hers, as they had done many times in the spring. Joy welled in her when she saw him a block away and when they embraced on meeting. Back at his new room, smaller and less attractive than the old attic, he grasped her in a tight embrace and planted a hard kiss on her mouth.

It was so unlike previous ones that she pulled away and exclaimed involuntarily, "No, no—this isn't right!"

"Yes it is—it is if you think it is."

He misunderstood her, she knew, whether deliberately or not, but as on the evening of his return she found herself tongue-tied. She could not ask what was wrong and strained to make light conversation. Underneath, the boiling terror of the first reunion took over.

They walked to a movie and he took her home on the bus. Twice after that, in the next week, they went to parties like those in the past spring. Sol regained some of his exuberance, but none of it was directed at her. He did not call her nor she him after that.

So Siggy had been wrong. Her first instincts had been absolutely right. Grief engulfed her, pain unlike any she had ever known stayed with her night and day. With it came contempt for herself, a raging anger she nursed as an antidote.

How could she, a psychology major, have so deluded herself with wish fulfillment beliefs! For one evening she had become a composite of Juliet and Joan of Arc—deathless love and divine revelation all rolled into one—the handsome, elegant lover divinely ordained specifically for her! Not bad, not bad for a girl of quintessential mediocrity—a girl lacking beauty, talent, or first-class brains. What had she to give the beautiful Sol, when other girls had so much more! She gritted her teeth and flung the grief away. She would not move into the popular torch song model, "Moanin' low, my sweet man I love him so…" But the heavy, heavy heart was there every morning and night, and she could not stop remembering that Sol had loved her. As for wish fulfillment, never in her life had she yearned for contact with the divine, quite the contrary. That had been thrust upon her from somewhere deep in her unconscious. She could not deny the impact of its reality, but then, the most deluded believe implicitly in their delusions. It had seemed totally real because she had shared it with Sol, but the sharing was also her own delusion. Thinking she could "unscrew the unscrutable," she mocked herself.

So she worked, liking it, saw friends and continued to be financially dependent on her sister, trying sporadically for a full-time job. Siggy took her out occasionally, but former suitors had disappeared except for one who asked her to marry him. She had never even kissed him. She was shocked, and it confirmed her belief in the power of self-delusion. Surely he must have felt some response in her that matched his own feelings, but there had been none. So with Sol:

Although he had loved her to some degree, the intensity of her feelings for him had been unmatched.

On a date with Siggy, he asked her, "What was it about him that hit you so hard? I know he's handsome and personable, but he always seemed rather juvenile, especially in comparison with you."

"I don't know how to describe it, Siggy. You'll find it hard to understand because it's so extraordinary, involving something absolutely, overwhelmingly unique in my experience—and in that of anybody I've ever known."

He persisted, and she described as best she could the events of the evening preceding their spring day trip and her subsequent life in the new and magical world.

"It sounds crazy, doesn't it? I've never told anyone about it."

"No—not really," he answered slowly. "To tell you the truth I had a not dissimilar experience once, a long time ago, which I never told anyone about, either. By the way, have you ever read William James' *The Varieties of Religious Experience*?"

No, she hadn't.

"You should."

"Can you tell me what happened to you?"

"I had just turned fourteen, the summer before my last year in high school. I was heavy into competitive long-distance swimming. The day before this thing happened, I had dropped out of a race after 12 miles, too exhausted to go on. I was bitterly disappointed in myself for that and with my life generally. Although I was popular at school, with teachers because of my grades and kids because of my athletic ability, a kind of prodigy, I knew no girl would ever love me because of my bad leg. I wanted to die; I knew I had to die. That evening I swam out to sea, intending to keep going until I drowned. I don't know how far I swam or for how long. I was getting very tired. Then suddenly every fiber of me seemed to be brilliantly illuminated and a kind of voice from somewhere said with total authority, 'Go back. I need you. I love you.' Something like that. I was transformed and managed to get back to the beach." There was a long pause. "And here I am, honey." He laughed, took her in his arms, and kissed her.

Ah, Siggy, Siggy—to know so much, to have such depths of understanding. How lucky she was to have a friend and admirer of such extraordinary quality.

Just before New Year's she sent Sol a card: Happy New Year, no bad feelings. A week later she answered the phone. It was Sol! Her heart leapt, she could hardly speak. "Can I come over?" By some miracle, she was alone in the house, and he was at the door in twenty minutes.

"How was it at the North Pole?" she asked, truly at a loss for words, as she had been in the fall when he returned to her.

"Not so great." A long pause, then, "I want to tell you that last summer, at camp, something terrible happened. My father had to learn about it and it was hell!"

"What happened, what happened!" she exclaimed, astounded.

"I can't tell you. I won't talk about it. But I want to see you again."

They went for a walk over the crunchy snow, under the star-studded winter sky. A walk—the way they had spent much of their time the previous spring. They talked of what each had been doing during their time apart, his courses, her training work at the social agency, no real job for her yet in that depression year. All the while her mind was occupied with the mystery of what had happened to Sol, her feelings a jumble, but mostly joy.

"There's a dance at the school next Saturday night. Will you go with me?" he asked when they parted at her door.

Of course she would. When he kissed her good night, all the joy of the previous spring returned.

The dance at school was a disaster. Five or six new friends met at a still different new room, with roommate, at the boardinghouse. Sol was in highest spirits. Nobody paid any attention to Mimi. A brief encounter with one tall young man held no significance at the time, except to seem ridiculous. Only years later, in retrospect, did she think of it as a straw in the wind that might explain Sol's difficulty.

As she stood gazing off into space, not really seeing anything, this youth pointed to a calendar on the wall next to her, a picture of a pretty girl, and said, "You probably thing she is very pretty, don't you?"

"I guess so," answered Mimi. "Don't you?"

"No, I don't. I think the female form is ugly—all those stupid protuberances. Only the male body is beautiful—straight, clean, graceful lines."

Mimi laughed, thinking he was joking, although certainly in no agreeable way. She moved off and didn't give the exchange another thought. At that time she knew nothing of homosexuality, despite having read several volumes of Proust's *Remembrance of Things Past*, fascinated by the endless convolutions of his introspection, and assuming that Albertine was a woman, as described. The very idea that persons of the same sex could be lovers would have seemed preposterous to her. It was a long time before she learned about Proust and before she accepted the reality of homosexuality.

In any case, at the dinner dance, Sol continued to ignore her, his high spirits directed only at the new friends. She was crushed and heartbroken all over again. In the days that followed, when he did not call, her mind was totally preoccupied with speculation over the "terrible thing" that had happened to Sol last summer. What on earth could it have been—a brawl with a camper or colleague or superior? Drunkenness? Theft? Refusal of duties? Nothing she could think of, knowing Sol, could appear to be totally devastating. The truth was, of course, that she knew little of his family or external circumstances, but she believed she knew him through his inner psyche, and that was all troubled goodness and generosity.

At the end of the week she called and asked to see him. They went for a walk.

She asked again, "Please tell me what happened last summer."

"I can't, and I won't!" He was angry.

"What did you mean when you said you wanted to see me again? It wasn't to be like last spring, was it?"

"No, not like last spring."

They said good-bye at her door with a light kiss, and that was the last time.

Over the many years she followed his career sporadically through the college alumni magazine. He became a psychiatrist, a full professor at one of the country's great university medical schools, married, had children; the name of his wife, a distinguished physiologist, appeared (as did Mimi's) in *Who's Who of American Women*. So if, as Mimi came to suspect, the camp incident had to do with a homosexual episode, it certainly did not spoil his life.

A long cold winter—1934–35: Siggy saw her occasionally; he also dated a couple of other girls she knew, and drove to New York some weekends. In April he told her that Elly was engaged to a man in New York. In May he told her that Elly had broken the engagement. In the first instance he did not seem very sad, nor very glad in the second, and Mimi decided that Elly was more of a hobby than a pursuit. It was the first time since the age of thirteen that Mimi was not a little in love with some youth who was a little in love with her. She tried to comfort herself with a rhyme, as she often did:

> My doleful song is slow and sad,
> My step is slow and lonely—
> How different would be my song
> Had I a one-and-only.

The most important event happened in June. She got a job, and not just any old job, either. She was hired as a caseworker by the newly established Federal Emergency Relief Administration. So began a career that shaped her knowledge and view of the political economy for the rest of her days. Worries about the depression had had to do with her personal fate and those of friends and family, none of whom was facing utter destitution. Now she learned to deal with people whom unemployment had stripped of the very means of subsistence, along with many of their belongings which had been repossessed by creditors. Through her investigations they were able to obtain food, rent, utilities, and clothing which would keep them in life and dignity. It was not a simple job, and it absorbed her so completely that she stopped mourning. She also became self-supporting for the first time in her life. She moved into the apartment of her sister Molly and a roommate, and she paid her way.

David had written her from Paris a few times. He had given up his Ph.D. studies during the first year of his fellowship and taken a job as an Associated Press reporter. He was obviously enthralled with it. More than anything, he had always wanted to write. In June 1936, he wrote that he would be in New York over the summer, would call and want to see her. Life with him had become a kind of hazy memory to her.

Also in June 1936, Siggy called her upon his return from a trip to New York. "I have something important to tell you, and I want to make a date for tomorrow evening dinner."

They went to an attractive restaurant-bar, a former speakeasy. Siggy was glowing.

"Honey, I broke off with Elly completely over the weekend. I told her I was going to ask you to marry me. Will you marry me?"

Not once had she ever thought of marrying Siggy, and she was stunned into silence.

"Will you? Will you? I've realized over the past few months that I love you more than anyone in my life. I know you love me, too. I may not be your handsome fairy-tale prince, but what we have is real."

Yes, it was real, the most real relationship she had ever had with any person, male or female, layered into depths of his understanding, her admiration, and the sheer pleasure of their companionship.

"I do love you, Siggy," she finally spoke, "but marriage? I just don't know. I've never thought about it."

He took it for granted that she had said "yes," and in a way so did she. How could she not marry him? He was the most superior human being she had ever known. Compared with him, the men who had wanted her seemed incomplete, lacking solidity, lacking the sure life force that emanated from his every word, every move. She knew, too, that her own quality was inferior, that he was "too good for her," that if it weren't for his bad leg he might have sought a more accomplished girl. And just that bad leg was a source of concern to her. Siggy's physical competence was actually greater than that of most men, but appearances count, too. She remembered one instance with Sol. He had arranged to pick her up at closing time at the department store where she was working one Saturday. As she watched him walk across the floor of the coat department, a glow of rapture enveloped her: Look, look, you drab mortals (the middle-aged saleswoman nearby) in this drab underworld, look at the Greek god who has descended from Olympus to rescue me from your toils. Could she eliminate the possibility of a similar appearance ever again in her life? For this ambivalence she chided herself: She had never cared enough for physical beauty to value it equally with character and personality.

In this context, a related event took place. Siggy attracted her physically, that she knew, and shortly after the proposal they went to bed in his apartment, the first time they were nude together. He left the bed at one point, and he saw her watching him as he returned, bad leg out of brace, needing a hand to move it.

"What do you think, honey? Is it maybe better to own an authentic Greek sculpture, even if part of it has been battered by time and circumstance, than a contemporary undamaged one?"

The aptness of the metaphor, and the self-confidence it exhibited, the result of the magnificent torso he had built over the years, burned into her. Yes, of course—this was Siggy, nothing hidden, openness and competence guiding his life.

In July, she and Siggy hunted for an apartment and shopped for furniture. Siggy had a bonanza: His mother had invested some of his money in stocks and made a profit which he would spend on the apartment and a honeymoon cruise to Bermuda. Mimi had no money, nor did her parents, and she did not even intend to tell them about the marriage. There was a complication: Molly objected to her seeing Siggy. Before Mimi came to live in R_____ , Siggy had taken Molly out a few times, and she had apparently fallen in love with him. She had even asked Mimi not to see him, but Mimi had refused to comply with such an unreasonable request. Siggy was her friend, and Molly's contact was incidental and totally a result of that friendship. But now she could not even bring herself to tell Molly about the marriage. Rachel knew and even helped Mimi shop for furniture. It was awkward and painful, but Molly had grown more and more neurotic over the years, and they could not satisfy her tearful demands and complaints. Molly would spend the summer with her parents. There would be no wedding celebration, neither Mimi nor Siggy's parents would be invited—just notified after the fact. They would just get married at Rachel's house.

All of this, plus the original ambivalence, kept Mimi in a state of anxiety. David was in New York, his first return home from Paris, and wrote that he wanted very much to see her. A former date with whom she had had a brief romance during the last term of college had suddenly started writing to her. He invited her to spend a weekend visiting friends of his in a New York suburb. Torn and disturbed, she arranged with Siggy to drive to New York over a long weekend. Siggy's parents, whom she had met previously and who seemed to approve of her, would be away, but she would stay at their apartment Friday night. Saturday she would see David, then stay overnight with a cousin, and on Sunday be picked up by Henry, the other young man, to be driven to Long Island to visit his friends. Complicated plans, utterly unlike her ordinary unperipatetic life: She was driven not by choice but by an overpowering malaise to revisit much of her past.

The weekend was even more unsettling than the planning. She and Siggy arrived late Friday night, slept together, and made love in his bed. The next noon she met David at his hotel. It was a joyous reunion. His enthusiasm overflowed as he regaled her with nonstop accounts of his newspaper work. Welcomed, amused, and beguiled, being with him felt utterly natural. They made love in his room, and that, too, felt just like herself.

Still in his bed, however, she told him, "I'm going to marry Siggy Braun."

"What!" he exclaimed. "Of course you're not."

She could say no more.

On Sunday, Henry picked her up in his car to drive to visit his friends. En route he remarked, "I was so surprised summer before last to see all those letters from you to Sol Rosen. Why on earth were you writing to him?" His tone was deprecating.

Her heart leapt.

"I never knew you were at that camp!"

"Sure, I was a counselor there for years."

The two had lived in the same fraternity house at college, but she was astonished to learn they had been together that fateful summer. Here was her chance for real information. Instead, a coldness froze both mind and feeling. She was seized with only one thought: She would not discuss Sol with him. For the rest of her life she could never understand why she had refused to follow this lead. It was quite irrational, against any kind of good sense or even ordinary curiosity, but there she was—totally blocked, unable to hear or speak a word about Sol.

Nor was this her only folly on this visit which became progressively more bizarre and herself unreal. Henry praised the couple, their hosts, extravagantly: They were models of wisdom and achievement to him. The wife, in particular, was a sympathetic advisor vis-à-vis a career for him; he didn't intend to keep on working in his father's wholesale business. He particularly wanted Mimi to meet her. Mimi was cordially welcomed, but she was surprised at the sharp-tongued, small, and not pretty woman who questioned her at length about her life, and not very sympathetically. Mimi responded as agreeably and openly as she could, all the while wondering, why, why had Henry, this relative stranger, wanted them to meet? In private, the woman praised Henry highly, particularly his extraordinary good looks. The girls at the sorority house had been well aware of that and congratulated her when he took her out. It was just after the break with David. The relationship had disturbed her: He was very attractive physically but not interesting as a person, and when he stopped calling, she had been relieved. Ridiculous though it seemed, Mimi had a feeling that the wife, perhaps in love with Henry herself, was inspecting Mimi as a possible mate for him. She was confused and distressed. That did not stop her, however, from sitting on the living room sofa with Henry after the couple had gone to bed and for two hours engaging in close embrace and kisses with him. All the while, a raging internal disturbance took place over her behavior: who was she, what on earth was she doing?

The next day they drove back to New York with little to say to each other—two strangers. When Siggy picked her up at her cousin's for the trip home, joy overwhelmed her. It was as if she had awakened from a terrible nightmare into a beautiful reality.

A test, a test—some kind of stupid test she had imposed on herself to confirm her decision. This became the way she looked back on that weekend for the rest of her life, forgiving herself for the seemingly wanton behavior.

Marriage

Marriage

Marriage

How marriage suited them! Siggy gave up his athletic and private golf club memberships to save money and spend leisure with Mimi. She loved homemaking: They had a six-day-a-week maid who cleaned house and prepared and served dinner and cleared away afterward. She drove him to his laboratory, took the car to work, and picked him up in the evening, sometimes stopping to market. It seemed she had been created for this life. The only stricture was to consult him before making dates with friends, of whom they had many. Evenings at home he spent at his desk, poring over work, while she contentedly read a miscellany of fiction and information. They lived very well indeed, materially and emotionally. The ghost of Sol came back to her in dreams sometimes, to her joy wanting her back, but she shook him away in the morning, unreal as in life.

Siggy continued to play golf on public courses. He was very good at it, despite an unorthodox stance, and wanted Mimi to play with him.

"You need to take some lessons," he told her. "It's a great game—as they say, good, mild exercise which keeps you outdoors. It's not so mild for me, because just walking around the course gives me a workout and helps keep me in shape, especially now I've given up the gym."

"Do you mind giving up the gym? You could still do it, you know. I certainly wouldn't mind."

"No, in a way I'm relieved to be through with it. It was a heavy taskmaster all through my youth. I've outgrown both the need and the pleasure. And I need the time for work—and to be with you and do things around the apartment." He put his arm around her as they sat on the couch and kissed her. It was true, he had household projects and had set up a kind of shop in the basement where he would design and build bookcases, modern style (later known as art deco) to match their furnishings. Carpentry was another of his talents about which she had known nothing.

Mimi took a few golf lessons from a pro and then practiced on the driving range where Siggy coached her. Many a weekend was spent on the course and many an evening on the driving range. She had no natural facility. The only sport she had ever enjoyed was swimming and the only application to games was in gym class, which she hated.

One evening at the driving range, as they practiced side by side, her frustration over her efforts came to a boil. Her hands were sore, her back ached. Why on earth was she exhausting her body and her self-regard in this stupid effort which returned no progress? Yes, occasionally the driver clinked cleanly against the ball and lifted it perhaps a straight hundred yards. Most often the ball hit the ground a few yards off, to the left or to the right. So it was on the course, and as for her short game and putting, they were totally inconsistent and unreliable. When she kept score it was likely to be some hundred for nine holes!

"I'm through!" she called to Siggy, and stalked to the car.

When he joined her shortly afterward he asked, "What is it? What's the matter?"

"What's the matter? The matter is I hate this game. My hands are sore, my whole body is sore—and for what? I can't hit that damn ball right and you know it! I've been trying and trying and trying and I just can't do it anymore! I'm so humiliated!" She was crying.

"Trying!" he exclaimed. "You haven't begun to try! You don't know what trying means! And as for being humiliated, the last thing in the world to be humiliated about is learning to do something new. The only thing that's humiliating is being unwilling to learn!"

They drove home in silence. She was angry—perhaps the first time she had ever been angry at him: so unsympathetic, so demanding. She couldn't believe it.

No further reference to the incident was made by either of them but it lingered long in her mind, and eventually a great light dawned upon her: of course, of course—this was the answer. This was the source from which flowed his many abilities, his confidence and sense of self. That old adage, damn it: If at first you don't succeed, try, try again! Not just a bromide for impatient children, it embodied a vital message she had never understood. All her life she had done what came easily, turning away from effort that diminished her ego or her pride, seeking reassurance from approval and affection. If genuine achievement was wanted, it was necessary to concentrate tirelessly on learning how. She never discussed the new insight with Siggy, but it sparked a whole new way of looking at herself and evaluating her activity which went on for the rest of her life. And she kept playing golf, which actually did more good than harm, although it became obvious she would never be a real golfer.

They were friends with a half dozen or more young couples. A monthly three-table duplicate bridge game formed one of their social events. Siggy and Mimi played partners and concentrated on improving their game. It was amicable, with agreement on bidding conventions, hand play, and defensive techniques. Siggy did not much enjoy evening gatherings where politics, economics, and foreign affairs were discussed, however. When he himself spoke, it was to a point where his fund of knowledge was accurate and his reasoning sound. This certainly was not true of many others, and he quickly grew bored with off-the-cuff opinions and irrelevant references. Not one of the others—young scientists, lawyers, struggling small business people—had his photographic memory or encyclopedic information framework. Through his years of lonely recovery from polio he had developed the habit of reading encyclopedias. To search authentic sources, not just in science but in any field, was automatic with him, and it seemed that anything he had ever learned was ready at hand when a discussion called for it. Not that he held forth at length: information and opinion were pithily expressed with great clarity. Mimi listened to him with appreciation and pride. In their personal discussions, too, on any subject, he was the great clarifier.

Parenthood & War

Parenthood & War

Parenthood & War

On November 15, 1941, less than a month before Pearl Harbor, their daughter was born. Mimi quit her job early in the pregnancy, they rented a house, dismissed the maid for a twice-a-week cleaning woman, and Mimi started learning to cook, which went well after the morning sickness tapered off. She enjoyed all the preparation and anticipation.

The delivery, however, was another matter. She had not known it was possible to suffer such agony, with no anesthesia until the very end. The baby was delivered by forceps, and Mimi was sore for months afterward. They could not afford a regular nursemaid except for the first two weeks. Siggy had never had routine domestic responsibilities, and child care was quite beyond him. The beautiful healthy baby, Lucy, brought little joy because her mother was in a constant state of exhaustion and confusion. Breastfeeding soon had to be supplemented by bottle formula, another chore, with weighing before and after each feeding.

Housekeeping in those days was totally different from the experience it became after World War II into the last half of the century. There were no synthetic detergents, no powerful insecticides, no automatic clothes washing machines or dryers, no dishwashers, no large home freezers nor bonanza of frozen foods in the supermarkets, no synthetic fabrics that needed no ironing. Looking back from the vantage point of the '90s, Mimi knew that she was one of the few persons still living who realized first hand how technology had revolutionized homemaking so that it became immeasurably less demanding. It also became less creative and rewarding. She believed that it was primarily the technological revolution, rather than Title VII of the Civil Rights Act of 1964, which sent women in droves into the workplace.

While Mimi was struggling with her new role, Siggy became more and more dissatisfied with his own job. Expected promotions and salary increases did not materialize. When Lucy was one year old, the search for another job he had been conducting succeeded. A small firm in Chicago, with new war contracts, hired him as director of research. The salary was twice his current one. He was elated. Leaving the baby with Rachel and a hastily hired nursemaid for a week, Mimi went with Siggy to Chicago to rent a place to live. His laboratory was in the southwest area, and because of gas rationing they needed to find a place near his work. The neighborhoods were drab and monotonous, row upon row of identical houses, in contrast to the charming, well-treed old place they had occupied. When the wind blew form the north, the stench from the stockyards filled the air. They found a relatively new and decent bungalow, however, and ultimately settled into it.

They had thought that his much larger income would ease their lives. It did not happen. She could not drive him to work, again because of gas rationing, and have the car. Nor could they do much recreational driving. Capable domestics had disappeared into war industry, laundries were unreliable because their help had followed the same route, washing machines were unavailable at any price. Mimi had a diaper service, but baby clothes had to be handwashed every day. A once-a-week domestic was all that could be found. Coal dust covered the furniture; dusting and vacuuming were a daily requirement to keep the house up to Mimi's standard. Mimi felt like a slave, especially since there were no family members or friends to lighten her burdens.

At the same time, she felt deep gratitude that the country was at last at war with the hideous Germany and often felt ashamed to be upset over personal troubles when Jews like herself had been hounded and lost everything. News of the death camps did not surface until the end of the war, but the persecutions that had were horrible enough.

Siggy, on whom she always counted for cheerful encouragement, if not actual help with child care and housekeeping, seemed to be overwhelmed by the responsibilities of his new job. He paid scant attention to her and Lucy, his evenings spent mostly in his den, poring over texts and experimental data. Mimi had not known he could be so grim.

Two major causes of her distress, however, were factors she could not have recognized at the time. The first was her nearly total dependence on the supposed expertise of psychologists and pediatricians, which she later came to think of as victimization. She worried constantly about her beautiful and intelligent baby's development. Every jot and tittle of the child's behavior was subjected to intense scrutiny, with constant references to the works of John B. Watson, Arnold Gesell, and other works on child care and development. Was this or that normal? What was she supposed to do about prolonged crying at bedtime, refusal of foods, shows of temper, clinging too much, refusing to play by herself? There had to be answers, but she could not find them. Babies should not be conditioned to expect constant attention, it was overstimulating. They should not be taken out into crowds for fear of infection. When adults gathered for any purpose, children should be left at home with baby-sitters. Not knowing any reliable baby-sitters in her new home, Mimi was afraid to get about on errands or evenings out. She did manage to hire a lovely schoolgirl two afternoons a week, but it was not enough. At age two plus, Lucy was sent off to nursery school, clinging and crying, two mornings a week. Mimi was continuously agonized because her child was not "normally" happy at all times.

She herself was no fun, either, constantly wracked by anxiety and the pressures of housework and child care. She expected Siggy to help her, was cross with him and he with her. At the end of his second year with his company, he took leave to work on some secret war project at the University of Chicago. During that year he secured another research position with a brand new group in another city, and they moved away.

The second cause of her distress she did not learn about until ten years after the fact, when Siggy told her, "That job was impossible. The owner had always been his own research director. His ideas and mine never meshed. I was on a hot seat I'd never felt before. You were miserable at home and there seemed nothing I could do about it. My only real thought about that was to make enough money so we could separate and I could support you!"

It shocked her to learn this so long after the fact. She had never for a moment considered leaving him, had never blamed him for her unhappiness, only felt that more help and companionship from him would lessen it. Through it all, she had been deeply grateful to be married to him. Never before nor after she married him had she met a man whose virtue and accomplishment matched his, nor one who was capable of such wholehearted, consistent devotion. Yet if he had so much as implied that he might want to separate himself from her, she might have thrust him away as she had previously done with others, and run, run—like the Gingerbread Man—from any threat to her self-regard.

It would have been a tragedy. Yet in today's world, where marriage and faithfulness are held in such low esteem, the experience she was recalling would very possibly have driven them apart. She shuddered at the thought. The years that followed led to a depth of mutual appreciation only lightly foreshadowed by the early ones. She gradually came to understand that his absorption in work was required for the excellence with which he performed all tasks, that excellence on which so much of her love and respect was based. It was a kind of persistent industriousness, calmly undertaken, which had been unknown to her or any member of her family. Planned time was of the essence to him, and when he made time to be a jolly or supportive companion, he matched the best of them. In turn, she believed he loved her in considerable measure for the easy sociability which was necessary to her. Certainly he encouraged and was interested to hear about the various activities and people she found along the way. He cooperated fully with well-spaced (in terms of his work schedule) parties, at home and elsewhere, and going to concerts, operas, theater, museums—all events where their tastes fortunately coincided. He was, furthermore, the best of hosts.

Letter to Her Husband

Letter to Her Husband

Letter to Her Husband

August 18, 1997

Darling Siggy,

It's a little over four years since I wrote the letter that prefaced this account. Four years to write such a little bit! Today was our 61st anniversary. I have talked to you each of the 4 x 365 days which have elapsed. I have written other letters and a ream of thoughts. I don't believe I can go on with a more or less chronological narrative of our life together or my life since you left. I never expected to be here still: How I prayed for death—and expected it—in those first four years. I was sick in body and soul. I was sure some ailment would take me. I knew, however, that suicide was out of the question because of the devastating effect it would have on the children and everyone else connected with us.

One night about two years ago, I was especially distraught. The breast cancer had returned—after thirty-three years—on the chest skin. I had severe anemia, was always exhausted, and feared I might have to face nursing care, either in a hospital or at home. The purgatory my life had become threatened to turn into an actual hell.

I was in bed, couldn't sleep, and I called to you, "Oh, Siggy, Siggy, I am so desperate. What shall I do?"

Your voice, it was like your very voice, echoed through me, "Courage, honey, courage!"

Of course! As my panic subsided, I realized it was the way you had always handled difficulties: thought, planning, work, and above all courage to follow through. You once told me that your mother told you that of all the virtues, courage was the greatest.

I've steeled myself to plan what is within my power to do. Our doctor insisted that I get radiation for the cancer. If I left it alone, it would worsen and become unlivable yet not fatal. The radiation was brutal, with third-degree burns, and it wizened me like a prune. It's healed to a tender chest which doesn't let me wear a bra, but I've rigged up some padding which lets me look halfway decent when I get dressed. The anemia has been treated well enough so I have some energy again. There are other physical failings, but I still keep the house and garden okay, handle my own finances, drive the car, visit with neighbors, entertain at home and out occasionally. Memory loss dogs me—can't remember names, numbers, new words, even old ones come and go. Oh, your memory! I counted on it always, but what a comfort it would be today!

The most amazing good fortune I have is Rory. When we rather whimsically named her Aurora, for light, as we did with Lucy, I never dreamed that she would become the comfort, the light, of my old age. Rory gives me many weekends, and she calls me every night.

As I write, I keep wondering: Could it be possible your consciousness actually exists somewhere in this mysterious creation and knows what goes on with me? Emerson said, "The blazing evidence of immortality is our dissatisfaction with any other solution." How I want to believe it and do believe in some kind of immortality but find it hard to think there's a total individual survival. I keep remembering the dream you related to me the second year of our marriage. You were boarding a train, you thought I was right behind you, but when you looked back I had disappeared. You ran frantically through the cars looking for me. A conductor stopped you, kindly sat you down, and explained, "You are dead, your wife is still alive, you must sit here and go to sleep, and when you awaken she will be there next to you." So it happened, and when I arrived I told you about all the wars and revolutions all over the world since you had left—and that our *son* headed a worldwide government!

Are you sleeping on the train, waiting for me? Metaphors, metaphors—since time began humans have dreamed up metaphors to explain life on earth and the hereafter. My own favorite is like the near-death accounts people relate these days: The spirit, or consciousness, hovers over the dead body first, then traverses a long dark tunnel toward a brilliant, infinitely loving and welcoming light. In my imagination you will be there in the light at the end of the tunnel. We will go on together to whatever experience awaits us.

Are you asleep, waiting for me on the train? I would prefer you to be awake, hearing me, but who knows? I only know that my loneliness overwhelms me, but that I must carry on and do the best I can with the life still left to me. "Noblesse oblige," I tell myself. Having received the gift of your nobility all those years, I owe it to both of us to live accordingly. Recently I was reading Montaigne, and he said that you cannot judge the whole of a man's life until you know how he died. I will try to die well.

As for the rest of this account, I think I will try to hit some high spots but not necessarily in any particular order.

All my love,

Mimi

Transcendence

Transcendence

Transcendence

The memory of Sol and the paradise she had lived in with him for three months occupied Mimi's subconscious for all the following years. However illusive it may have been, she had known paradise before the fall, and subsequent time was lived in paradise lost. So it had been ordained for mortals since time began. Instead of grieving, one should be grateful to have caught even a glimpse of it. How many people, she wondered, have been granted such a boon?

This set her off on a long search for accounts of personal religious experiences. She finally read William James' *The Varieties of Religious Experience* and was enthralled to recognize parallels to her own sudden, totally unsought exaltation in the direct presence of divinity. The book was a marvel of brilliant, eloquent, and objective observation. Why wasn't it required reading for every inquiring mind, especially for contemporary followers of the thought of Marx and Freud: Marx and his "opiate of the people," designating religion as a purely political tool with which the powerful oppress the powerless; and Freud, to whom it was just another wish fulfillment delusion? Call it what you will, this sudden, overwhelming revelation of one's supreme, overriding, essential belonging to the whole magnificent, mysterious universe brought a kind of pure joy and gratitude no other human experience could match. It was the basic inspiration of great spiritual leaders throughout history, she believed, and it represented an absolute fundamental of the human psyche.

The prophets in the Bible, from Moses on, were no doubt inspired by such experience, but they were so tied in with an anthropomorphic deity, so many commandments and proscriptions, important and trivial, so much political confrontation, that the essence of religious experience never comes clear. It certain never had to Mimi, nor, she believed, to the vast majority of Jews. This might be true of Christians as well.

Almost by accident, she began to read Hindu writings: the *Dhammapada* of Buddha, the *Bhagavad Gita*, and some more contemporary works; *The Synthesis of Yoga* and others.

"You know," she told Siggy one evening, "Now I know how come our forefather Abraham latched onto the idea of one God to replace all the tribal gods of the time. In his travels, one day he sat down in an oasis beside a traveling Hindu. These two spiritually inclined men had a wonderful discussion in which the Hindu described to Abraham the essence of the *Bhagavad Gita*, who knows, maybe even read it to him if it had been printed and adequately translated at the time, like the Sir Edwin Arnold one I have! Sudden illumination came to Abraham—of course, of course, there was the answer to all his spiritual doubts and strivings!"

"Yeah?" asked Siggy. "How do you figure it?"

"If you have time, I'll read you the *Bhagavad Gita* right now—or at least the most significant parts of it."

This she did, and Siggy, who was basically more religious than she despite no formal practice of it, understood why she had invented this little fable of her own.

Siggy had not been brought up Jewish—no synagogue, no bar mitzvah, nothing. Although both his parents were Jewish, they had siblings who married non-Jews. It was a close family but completely secular. Yet when Lucy started school, Siggy had gladly agreed that they should join a temple and send Lucy to Sunday school. They themselves attended services occasionally, and Siggy was glad to learn something about his ancestral religion. Both children stayed with it until confirmation, although for the most part reluctantly. Mimi did not follow Jewish observances at home except for an occasional Friday night, sporadic holidays, and always a Passover seder. Neither of them found Jewish friends more compatible than non-Jews. It was a matter of personality as well as not having grown up in a Jewish milieu; in her case because hers had been the only Jewish family in their small town, and she the only Jewish child in school. A small Jewish community existed in a nearby town, and she had gone occasionally to meaningless services in Hebrew. Her mother kept a kosher house, despite difficulties, her father said daily prayers with phylacteries, but none of it related to her life.

In any case, her reading in comparative religion went on, with emphasis on personal religious experience. Jewish mysticism echoed the search for this, but the Kabbalah was impenetrable, and other philosophers not very illuminating. Only the Hindu writings reached her. She undoubtedly would have needed a guru and group practice to gain serious emotional sustenance from this, just as she might have gained it from some Jewish group exploring its version, but she had no ready access. Her group activity turned in another direction completely.

Always underneath daily living, however, remained the certainty that a separate spiritual world existed. She did not expect that she would ever reach Nirvana in this life, never again, but it was somewhere in another realm waiting for her. In the meantime, one must follow as closely as possible the major precepts for moral living as enunciated in all the major religions. It was a worldly way to stay close to divinity; it provided its own satisfactions. "Virtue is its own reward," even if one could get more euphoria, however fleeting, from two ounces of hundred-proof bourbon.

Progress:
Civic Responsibility
Civic Responsibility

Civic Responsibility

Siggy's new job with a small private research group in Washington, D.C., to which they moved in early 1945, suited him well: His colleagues were first-rate scientists, and they worked on contracts mostly from federal agencies. His parents lived there, his father a medical officer in a federal establishment. For the first two years they rented a dumpy apartment, found with difficulty because of the war housing shortage, but then bought an attractive house with the help of a loan from his parents.

When the bomb dropped on Hiroshima in August 1945, Siggy exclaimed, "So that's what it was all about!"

"What do you mean?"

"Well, you remember that I worked on a special war project at the University of Chicago? This was it! Although I never knew it was a bomb!"

"Really? How could that be? What did you think it was?"

"Not sure, everything was so compartmentalized, but I figured it had to be some kind of super fuel—an enormous power source. They sure managed to keep a bomb a big secret!"

Although Siggy's specialty was not nuclear physics, he under-stood its science. He was glad for the later development of nuclear power and believed its hazards could be kept under control. And whatever the horrors of the bomb, he knew that the Nazis would have tried to develop it and used it with abandon.

In any case, the horror of the war, the Cold War, and their aftermath was not the horror with which Mimi involved herself personally for the next twenty-five years. The horror at her doorstep when she enrolled Lucy in public school kindergarten became all too vivid. The elementary school for Negro children was two blocks from their home, that for whites six bocks away, and Lucy was sent to the latter. Mimi had never faced legal segregation; she had worked with Negro social workers in her agency. "Those damn southerners" had seemed far away—yet here in the nation's capital it became an intimate part of her daily life.

Aurora was born in 1948, but while Mimi was still pregnant she joined and became active in the organization that would work tirelessly to end segregation, promote integration, and foster government programs to combat the destitution and poverty that afflicted city blacks. Aurora's birth and infant care were easy, thanks in part to Dr. Spock and his revolution in infant care theory.

For twenty years Mimi gave the best of her mind and effort to the league. She learned about government in its study groups. The women she worked with enlightened and sustained her. Digging their way through issues, policies, bills, budgets, and lobbying legislators and testifying at hearings, they educated themselves more thoroughly than any college courses might have done. In retrospect, she knew that these were kinds of women who were now working as professionals, thanks to the women's movement. She and her co-members had been for the most part women with children with husbands who supported them. They worked in the public interest as a wellspring of democracy.

The meeting of minds and the teamwork that evolved in the process gave Mimi friends of superb quality. A course in group dynamics helped her achieve confidence to take leadership roles: committee chairwoman, board member, discussion leader, president, speaker of testimony.

Siggy listened and discussed with her the many issues with which the group grappled. At times he calmed down some of her intensity, for which she was grateful. His quick grasp of the dimensions of a question enhanced their conversation. The women she worked with were fine, but often it was Siggy who illuminated and helped her clarify thoughts and plans.

In 1963, at the height of the civil rights and antipoverty movements, she was stricken with breast cancer, and a mastectomy was performed. Despite the trauma, she appreciated—and was astonished by—the concern and care she received from Siggy, from her twice-a-week domestic, and from friends and colleagues. As soon as possible she returned to the load of organization work she had undertaken, although the march on Washington that summer occurred a bit too soon for her to join it with her group.

She expected to die. Her sister Rachel had died three years earlier after a long bout with metastasized breast cancer. Molly had died six years before that from stomach cancer. Instead of fear or apprehension, however, she was seized by strange exhilaration. If I'm going to die, she thought, I'll give myself to this work, something infinitely worthwhile, without having to worry about my future. It was a kind of farewell to the personal anxieties that had pervaded her life. When the five-year period during which metastases were to be expected finally expired, there was relief, but the exhilaration died.

In any case, work hard she did, taking on the presidency of the organization under a kind of time and thought pressure she had never known. When her term was up, concomitant with the five-year span of possible recurrence of the cancer, she was given an album with a dedication that read in part:

"How deep is the pride all of us feel to have been privileged to work with you! Your exemplary leadership inspired each of us to put forth her best efforts to try to match the standards which you set. The pursuit of excellence characterized your entire administration. It marked everything you did. Every letter, article, speech, and piece of testimony that left your desk bore the stamp of excellence."

There was more. She never looked back at this or shared it with anyone during subsequent years. Both her own efforts and the body politic slid backward from that high point. Looking at it in 1997, she knew that her own work had been sparked by a unique personal energy, and that the goals sought by her colleagues and the politics of that time had suffered badly in the intervening thirty years. The civil rights movement had been a success, it was true, despite important gaps, but the antipoverty effort, along with governmental concern for it, had tumbled backward. Instead of government for the people, it had become government against them—punitive toward the poor, punitive vis-à-vis personal liberty, especially with the war on drugs, punitive toward consumers and labor with support of huge corporations and "privatization." It was a government lost to the prior efforts of the Teddy Roosevelt reforms, the FDR New Deal, and the Kennedy-Johnson antipoverty initiatives. The Vietnam war, the Cold War, the Watergate and Iran-Contra scandals, the Arab oil boycott—all turned both the body politic and the economy into a raging storm.

After the mastectomy, Mimi had somehow assumed that her sex life with Siggy would terminate. It did for about six months until he patiently and tenderly seduced her back into his bed. He told her she was beautiful, lovely, lovable, and acted accordingly. If anything, their encounters were better than before because she was so grateful to him. As in the old rhyme, it amused her to be crooked people.

> There was a crooked man who walked a crooked mile
> He found a crooked sixpence against a crooked stile
> He found a crooked cat which pleased his crooked spouse
> And they all lived together in a big crooked house.

Actually, their first kitten had been a rachitic foundling which had wandered into Siggy's laboratory. And the house before the latest one had been a split level with no symmetry whatsoever.

Elders

Elders

Elders

The most urgent responsibility parents will ever have, by definition of nature, is the bearing and rearing of their children. Whether or not they recognize and act on this fact consciously, it consumes them. So it was with Mimi and Siggy. Fortunately, as with other aspects of their life together, they were able to consider and act harmoniously on the broad decisions involved. Mimi did not want, however, to include in this account the complexities of the undertaking; that would require a whole other story. Suffice it to say that, despite some trauma and disappointment, both daughters grew up to become educated, conscientious, affectionate, and for the most part successful in reaching their objectives in life.

Siggy retired from his corporate job (his laboratory had been acquired by a big company some years before) at sixty-five, as required. Before that happened, however, he had lined up several spots where he could become a private consultant. He had no intention of retiring. Patiently and methodically he set up an office at home. Slowly the demand for his services grew, and in a few years he became very selective, choosing work that dovetailed with his expertise and people he liked to work with. He was happier than ever before in his life. Mimi was happy, too. With daughters successfully on their own, despite an assortment of problems, she found life with Siggy at home quite delightful. Many days they hardly saw each other between breakfast and dinner, he at his desk or telephone, she looking after household chores, doing errands, lunching with friends. She took responsibility for home maintenance so he would not be burdened and engaged in some civic activity, but that was not anything like the total immersion she had known in her middle years. It had exhausted her utterly. She thought, let younger women do it: Ironically, of course, they never did. They were too busy working at their professions.

Travel, mostly in connection with Siggy's work, entertaining at home, being entertained by friends, going out to concerts and shows, playing bridge—there were myriad things they enjoyed doing together.

They both suffered some ailments concomitant with aging. Siggy had cataract surgery on one eye before lens implants became standard, a weakening of his good leg, trouble getting adequate brace repair or a satisfactory new one, prostate surgery, a long healing time for a shoulder broken in a fall, some hearing loss in one ear with need for a hearing aid, elaborate bridgework on his teeth. None of it fazed him.

"It takes me a long time to get dressed these days!" Siggy announced cheerfully one morning as he came into the kitchen for breakfast. "All these spare parts!" They consisted not only of the brace, as of old, but the contact lens, the hearing aid, the removable bridge, an arch support and extra foot padding, and, in the last years, not just one, but two canes. He was clean shaven and wearing a shirt, tie, and sports jacket.

Mimi's ailments were mild arthritic and alimentary conditions about which she complained little. Instead, as he did, she used judgment about doctor's advice, sought and found ways of securing comfort. Siggy was an expert at this. His medical knowledge was vast, thanks to having lived with, discussed, and digested the expertise of his father, a brilliant research physician with much clinical experience in earlier years. Both had always maintained critical assessment of common medical practice. Because of this, they evaded the hypochondria and fear of so many elders, were able to adapt to actual disorders in an objective way and to go on about their business.

Only in retrospect was Mimi able to realize fully the appreciation Siggy had given her; she had taken so much for granted. Across the breakfast table, he would look up from the *New York Times* crossword, stare at her reflectively at first, then announce, "You're so beautiful!" And she in her seventies! "Oh sure!" she would say.

Or, on more than one occasion, he would burst out with "I'm so lucky," and then sing a few lines from an old song, "Lucky in love, lucky in love—what else matters if you're lucky in love..."

"You're so silly," she told him.

She might meow at him. Even cats like compliments.

She had been the lucky one. No one in her family—mother, father, sisters—had lived with this kind of optimism, love, *joie de vivre* in their later years. Neither had Siggy's parents, who had quarreled a lot, with his mother never seeming to find fulfillment in her husband's eminence. Nor did he, for he grew depressed with age despite maintaining a full consulting practice until his death at seventy-nine. Perhaps, Mimi thought, it was the near worship that she, in her mediocrity, accorded Siggy that made him feel "lucky in love."

Siggy's eightieth birthday was in July 1988. In March, Mimi began preparing for a special celebration, a surprise dinner for some fifty persons to be held at a nearby hotel. She targeted colleagues, past and present, and asked them to prepare a few words, "toast or roast." She and Rory wrote songs—she the words, Rory the music—to be performed. Nothing of the kind had ever been done for Siggy before. It was exciting and especially meaningful because no one close in his family had ever lived to be more than seventy-nine, and Mimi knew that he had not expected to live beyond this age, if that long. The party was a huge success.

A few days before the birthday Mimi answered a phone call in which an unfamiliar male voice asked to speak with Dr. Braun. Siggy talked for some time and came away with his face wreathed in smiles.

"It was a client, wasn't it?" Mimi asked.

"A man I'd never met or heard of. He got to me just through reading my book and journal articles! I think I can help him. We made a date to get together."

"A new client, hm? The best birthday present anybody could give you, isn't it?"

"Yeah—it's great to be loved!"

For several years he had been saying on occasion that his clients might not renew their contracts because of his age. They had done so, however, and here was a brand new one.

Another summer morning, across the breakfast table, he was reading a scientific journal and she the *New York Times*.

He looked up musingly and said, "You know, this is the most fascinating world. One could go on learning about it forever."

Her own thoughts, in response to the front page news, had been exactly the opposite: what a hideous world. The only solution to its oppression is to get out of it.

She could say nothing, only wish that she too were immersed in the search for scientific truth instead of looking at human disaster in the search for social and economic well-being.

Return to
Lost Loves

Return to
Lost Loves
Return to
Lost Loves

In April while Mimi was planning the birthday party, she received a call from David in New York. It was twenty-five years since she had last heard from him, when he had visited and had dinner with her and Siggy. He asked to have lunch with her alone. She made a date to take him to lunch at her club, wondering what could possibly have inspired this contact. He looked well, an erect old man of seventy-eight with gray hair and well-trimmed beard whom she would not have recognized. After a drink, lunch, and a catching up on current circumstances, they retired into one of the sitting rooms and spent the afternoon talking.

What had gone wrong with their love, he wanted to know. Why had she married somebody else? She was stunned by this inquiry, but since he seemed perfectly rational and articulate, she didn't ask for reasons for this retrospective but accepted it at face value, thinking he might be researching an autobiography, although he didn't say so. Apparently he had hoped and even expected some permanence would come from their affair. She told him, quite simply, that she had needed the total devotion he had been unable to give, mentioning his date with her sorority sister and wanting her to see other men, and that she had just given him up. He explained, quite unnecessarily, that his future had been too uncertain to make any commitment. He wanted to write to her. Would she answer? Yes.

She described the meeting to Siggy, and they agreed that first love has lifetime staying power. Siggy knew, however, that any old yearning of hers was not back to David. She had sometimes wondered whether Siggy had ever made contact with Elly—or with the professor's wife with whom he had had a serious affair when he was in graduate school. She had never asked nor had he ever mentioned their names during the more than fifty years of marriage.

A letter from David arrived in a week. They should have married, he said. He wouldn't have had his two sons nor she her present children, but they would have had fine children belonging to both of them. He apologized for his immaturity and insensitivity at the time. She was again amazed. She wrote back that his immaturity had been exceeded only by her own, that she never could have worked and taken care of children while he roamed Europe as a foreign correspondent, as his wife had done before, during, and after World War II until her untimely death from cancer. What a silly man he is, thought Mimi. She wrote that she had needed then, as she did now, the total devotion of Siggy, that whatever maturity she had gained through her long life had been learned for the most part exactly from Siggy.

David wrote one more time, an eloquent letter describing his unhappy childhood. She answered with appreciation, but heard no more. So much for deathless love! Three months later the college alumni news reported his death. No date or details were given: not the name of his second wife nor those of his sons, whom he had described to her. Mimi was shocked. Not his autobiography, then, but some terminal illness must have inspired the researching of his youth. How awful, how awful! He had given no inkling. She hadn't been unkind or indifferent, surely, but she hadn't been encouraging either. In the midst of planning Siggy's birthday party and also arranging for a trip, she had dismissed David's behavior as rather childish and strange. Now she conjectured that in extremis he had been reaching back to the happiest time of his life. She wished she had inquired sympathetically about his reasons for the retrospective.

The trip they were planning, in early June, was to Mimi's fifty-fifth college reunion. Neither of them had gone to one before, although they had visited the campus several times during the years. Mimi had more or less kept up with the lives of her two favorite sorority sisters through the alumni news, and in the winter she had contacted them about the reunion. Helen, who had so enthusiastically located Siggy in R_____ at the beginning, was delighted. They met, in the interim, on a trip to Washington by Helen and her husband and found that fifty-five years had not eroded a basic compatibility. Helen's husband, a retired M.D., fell easily into a friendship with Siggy.

An unspoken but impelling motive for Mimi lay in the possibility she might see Sol at the reunion. He had written amusing details of his life to the alumni news in recent years and attended reunions. Surprised that he kept up undergraduate friendship after so long an academic career elsewhere, she could not help but wonder whether he thought back to her, as she did to him, and perhaps hope for a meeting again. For her part, underneath the total absorption of busy life, a steady stream of wonder at the transformation she had undergone during the time with Sol was always there in her subconscious and the question remained, how far had it affected him? Was it possible that this late in life there could be an answer of sorts?

They met at the first class dinner. She had expected him to look like any other old man of seventy-five, all vestiges of youth gone, as had happened with others after so many years. He was already there when she and Siggy arrived, standing in the center of a listening group, animatedly holding forth. He was taller and broader than she remembered, and he was the handsomest seventy-five year old she had ever seen, not excluding Cary Grant!

Status quo ante! She was gripped by astonishment and confusion.

She and Siggy moved over to the group, received a rather perfunctory handshake and "how are you?" from Sol, after which he continued with his tale. At dinner they did not sit with him and his youngish wife, whom he had introduced as Amanda. But his wife had been Ruth.

"What happened to Sol's wife Ruth?" Mimi asked a classmate.

"Oh, Ruth died."

It was ridiculous how little she knew of the life of this man on whose account she had been "born again." Nevertheless, she was determined she would speak to him privately.

As they were leaving the room after dinner, she held him back. "Sol, can I talk to you for a few minutes?"

They sat at a table together while the others, including Siggy and Sol's wife, slowly filed out. She didn't know what she was going to say. First she told him she knew of his former wife's admirable career from an article she had read.

Then, emboldened by David's recent declarations, she said, "Sol, I just want you to know that the time we spent together all those years ago brought me a kind of happiness in a kind of world I never knew existed."

His eyebrows rose. It was obvious that he was taken aback, even embarrassed.

"I think," he answered slowly, "that women take these things more seriously than men."

That old cliché!

She realized that he had no doubt been pursued by women all his life. He was a man who engendered love. A fictional character, Gosta Berling, in the novel by Selma Lagerlof, was the only man she had ever met who resembled him.

"I know many people have loved you," she said soberly, "it's only that before I die," his eyebrows rose again, "I want you to know it was a unique kind of happiness." Somehow, that was all she could say.

"It meant something to me, too, you know," he answered.

"Yes. Well. I'm glad." She rose from the table. "I guess we should join the others."

Back in their room, Siggy smiled at her. "Well, did you get it out of your system?"

That was exactly what she had done. Siggy, so perceptive—never had she loved him more. She described the brief interview.

"He was wary. I think he was afraid I was slightly off my rocker —and that I would ask for a recapitulation and explanation, as David did with me."

Nonetheless, when she saw Sol at a distance later on, a kind of yearning possessed her briefly. Such is the power of the aesthetic, the power that beauty holds over love—and had throughout human history. Part of the process of natural selection, a biological basic it was, of course. Intellectualize it as one might, however, it stirred the heart, the mind, the senses, the soul.

Stroke -Death
Stroke -Death

Stroke - Death

She could hardly think back to it, let alone write about it, yet it haunted her continuously. Over and over again she thrust it from her consciousness. What was the use, it was done and done and done: Death ended life.

But not Siggy's! Mimi was supposed to die first.

He should have recovered from the stroke. He should never have suffered it. If she had not been so careless of his life, she would never have allowed him, old man of eighty, to fly on Tuesday to give a lecture, fly home Wednesday night, fly to New York Thursday morning to give a deposition on a patent suit for which he was the expert witness, fly home Friday morning, attend a concert with her on Friday night. Saturday morning at 7 A.M. she heard a thump in the bathroom, went to investigate, found him inert on the floor.

"I can't get up," he told her in a faint voice.

Telephone their internist, who arranged to meet them at the hospital emergency room with a neurologist. Telephone for a private ambulance. Telephone the children. Shriek at the ambulance men, over and over again, that they must go to the hospital where her doctors waited, not the nearest one as they said the law required. Before that, cover Siggy with a blanket, assure him help was on the way, kiss and reassure him over and over again that help was on the way. She was a madwoman, but she got him to the right hospital.

Oh yes, oh yes! The right hospital! The "best"! The "best" neurologist in the city who whisked him into a special intensive care unit for stroke patients, tied him up with a respirator and tubes. Only in the receiving room did she and the children have a chance to speak with Siggy; he was quietly cogent. Then away, away, away into the chamber of horrors where for nearly three weeks she was forced to sit in the hospital waiting room, with ten-minute intervals of sitting by his bed, holding his hand, talking to him but never knowing what he was thinking or feeling. He got pneumonia, his heart became irregular, a parade of specialists, with whom she never got a chance to talk, was called in. Each day the internist spent time with her, explaining that all this was necessary to keep the brain damage from spreading.

Day in, day out, she begged, "Take him out of that respirator, when can he come out?"

Finally, in the morning of the nineteenth day of hospitalization, their doctor called to say Siggy would be in a room by noon. She drove herself to the hospital in a frenzy of joyous anticipation. There he was—sitting in a wheelchair free of respirator and tubes.

She hugged and kissed and hugged and kissed and exclaimed with she knew not what. Finally she asked, "Oh honey, oh honey—how are you feeling, honey?"

He tried to speak, pointed to his throat, could not utter a word.

She knew about that from intimate contact with a friend who could not speak well after a stroke, used pad and pencil all the time. She whipped out a valentine she had brought him, turned the back of it in his hands, with a pencil, and said, "Your throat's constricted. Write."

He wrote unevenly: How are you feeling?

"Happy, happy! Can I get you something?"

"Water," he actually uttered.

"Oh yes, right away."

A nurse was standing nearby.

"He can't have water yet. He might choke. The doctor has to look at his throat."

Then, "He pulled the feeding tube out of his nose during the night. He said he wouldn't need it anymore."

Mimi was nonplussed. "If he wants water he must have it. Let's take care of it right away."

Another nurse standing in the doorway said something like, "The patient has rights, too."

Mimi was still hugging Siggy when his whole body began to shake and he suddenly collapsed into unconsciousness.

Without another word, orderlies appeared and wheeled him away.

"You stay here," said the nurse. "They are going to resuscitate him."

What period of time elapsed she did not know before a nurse appeared and told her, "They couldn't bring him back; he's dead. Come into the waiting room, the doctor will see you right away!"

Mimi babbled. She never remembered what words came out of her. Finally both the internist and the neurologist appeared and told her Siggy had died of a heart attack.

All alone, my darling, all alone in that devilish torture chamber they kept you in for nearly three weeks. All alone you must have had a heart attack in the night and pulled the tube out of your nose, knowing you were dying and would need it no more.

You died because you could no longer manage our own medical care as you had done all your life—you knew more than all the doctors. And I—I was too weak and stupid to make them set you free to use your brilliance to save yourself!

She knew many people who had recovered from strokes. With therapy they recouped many powers, some back to normalcy. This was what had been planned for Siggy: some time in a rehab hospital, then home to a revamped house so that his first-floor study would be a bedroom. It was all at ground level and held a full bathroom as well as a powder room. There would be money for whatever help was needed. Even if he had to give up the consulting, he could still do the theoretical writing and publish it as he had been doing anyway. With his determined and experienced mastery of physical ailments, he would not have been fazed. Nor would she.

Now it would never be. Nevermore.

Farewell

Farewell

Farewell

The living live on, and much as they may wish to fly away, they cannot!

So this half-person lives on, as she has written. She appears cheerful enough to family and friends, or so she believes, and makes a tremendous effort to be good company and helpful. Every evening she has a "happy hour"—two ounces of bourbon usually—by herself or with whomever will join her or invite her. Several neighbors do: couples in their forties, fifties, sixties in an alternating mix. Sometimes they have dinner together. Her place has a name: Mimi's Pub, outdoors on the patio in good weather, mostly in the kitchen when it's cold. They are intelligent and modestly successful and kind. And very jolly. Often the inner loneliness lifts completely in an explosion of laughter.

One thing she has refused to do is to be warehoused with other old women in some senior residence. She is familiar with them; she has eaten meals with friends there. The sea of surrounding old wrinkled faces, halting minds and bodies, nearly drowns her. In her own house and neighborhood, all ages, including children, come together. She lives as part of the future, not the dying past.

Bedtime is hard. Mornings are worse. All her life mornings were hard for her, even as a girl in school. Now they are impossible, but she cannot change her habits. With her meager breakfast and coffee, she looks over the *New York Times*. Gloom and doom all over the world are what it reports—the movement of huge power structures in conflict. She should break this habit and read instead from books which reflect the humanity and genius of world history, of which she has a large collection. The needs and accomplishments of the majority—ordinary decent people—are ignored, and the pursuit of power and wealth are celebrated in this medium. Morning pain from her own ailments, a fragile digestive system for which she takes medication, combines with the painful reading to create nausea and despair.

There is an old obligation to keep up with what goes on in the world which ties her to the paper, even though she knows well that it does not reflect real life. Unfortunately, there is no national leadership, no mass movement to counter the greed and will to power which dominate financial and government activities continuously reported. Television, radio, other papers, and most journals are worse. Certain journals do carry social criticism, but they are detached from wide readership or any source of action.

As for the popular culture on TV and in the movies, it is a total distraction from thought and respect for human decency; a massive clout on the head to focus attention on the commercials.

"Oh tempora, oh mores"—and of course Cicero was right, as his brutal murder attests.

So she finally gets busy to set her own lonely affairs in order and pursue, insofar as possible, the pleasing of family, friends, and herself.

Humility, humility, she tells herself. You cannot order the world, not even your own small pocket of it, with suburban sprawl thrusting you into a maelstrom of traffic and crowded malls so you won't even shop for yourself anymore!

Her good friend, retired from years in the state legislature, at eighty is still effectively fighting more highway construction which expands suburban sprawl. Unlike Mimi, however, she remembers the name and history of every person she has known, and the sequence of events and legislation come into her mind in an orderly way. Her capacious intellect, like Siggy's, still holds, along with her stubborn, placid perseverance. This goes on despite skeletal injuries which require her to use a walker. The greatest advantage she enjoys, nonetheless, is a devoted husband who at eighty-five is still perfectly cogent.

But Mimi must deal, in her own way with her own capabilities, with the loneliness and grief that dog her. At least she has refused her doctor's efforts to put her on antidepressants!

Memory lapses, physical tiredness, and discomfort keep her from engaging in political dialogue and action to counter the income inequality which has swallowed up the country in the past twenty years. She is no longer acquainted with others who care; only her reading informs her that about half the country earns less than it used to. She hasn't the energy or ability to seek and join forces with groups struggling against the dissolution of economic fairness. All she does is give money to some of them and to private charities, which never were and never will be the answer.

Excerpts from:

The Dhammapada of Buddha

The Dhammapada of Buddha

Old Age—Chapter XI

How is there laughter, how is there joy, as the world is always burning? Do you not seek a light, you who are surrounded by darkness?

Look at this dressed-up lump, covered with wounds, joined together, sickly, full of many schemes, but which has no strength, no hold!

The World—Chapter XIII

Look upon the world as you would on a bubble, look upon it as you would on a mirage: the king of death does not see him who thus looks down upon the world.

Come look at this world glittering like a royal chariot; the foolish are immersed in it, but the wise do not touch it.

The Way—Chapter XX

Death comes and carries off the man, honored for his children and his flocks…

Sons are no help, nor a father, nor relations; there is no help from kinsfolk for one whom death has seized.

A wise and well-behaved man who knows the meaning of this should quickly clear the way that leads to Nirvana.

The foregoing lines only give a flavor of the *Dhammapada* which has so affected Mimi. She does see the world as a bubble, a mirage, and she has ceased to care about the glitter. Yet while she lives in it, she must maintain the comforts she enjoys. Where else would she go? There is no ashram, no nunnery of companionable devotees available to her. She must manage the money so it can not only support her but be left for the children and grandchildren. There is no respectful place for beggars in this society—only sickness, misery, homelessness, and hate on the streets. It is family money, hard earned and saved by three hardworking generations, not secured through financial flim-flam; not a great fortune, indeed, but enough for comfort. Her offspring live well but not extravagantly, and they deserve to enjoy the security it will bring, just as Siggy and she did.

In truth, Mimi believes, the problem of poverty exists in some measure because too many millions have been too unlucky to enjoy the fruits of ancestral provenance; society as a whole, through government, must act *in loco parentis* in this regard. Inheritance taxes, in particular, would be more just if the money were spent on basic living needs of all the people. There should be a family allowance, as the European countries have, along with other benefits.

She is ready for death. If she could reach the equivalent of Nirvana on earth, she might not long for death. But she is not ready to give up all the earthly attachments, as defined by the Buddha, to reach this goal. She needs human affection and companionship; she needs the beauty of trees and garden which surround her home. Maintaining these take planning, work, and money.

Still, such a world view is there, but probably a person like herself can only hope to live in it at the point of departure from the earthly sphere. There simply has to be a parallel world to compensate for the hideous stresses of this one. It must be possible for every mortal to know the exquisite continuing joy, not just the snatches she once knew under nitrous oxide and in the thrall of youthful love.

Nevertheless, she has known a lifetime full of love. She believes her function now is to give it back. Everybody needs affection and appreciation. She can—and does—give that to many on an individual basis, even if she can no longer work toward a more caring society.

Letter to Her Husband

Letter to
Her Husband
Letter to
Her Husband

August 18, 1998

Darling Siggy,

Today is our sixty-second anniversary.

I have finished my account. I don't talk to you so often anymore, but a few nights ago, in a dream, you came through the door from the garage into the kitchen, as you used to do, and pure joy consumed me. I hugged and kissed you and exclaimed over and over again: of course you were here, of course, where else would you possibly be! Then I awoke and sorrow engulfed me. So it goes, beloved. That dream doesn't come as often as it used to. I know I must eschew it and look for a more all-encompassing hope, but my stubborn heart still clings.

Perhaps if I had found another man to love a little bit after you died, I could have escaped some of this grief. You would have been glad, I know, for any happiness I could find. You were never jealous of my lesser loves. But where on earth could I have found anyone? Old widowers are few, old widows abound, and the men have an age range of as much as fifty years from which to choose! I certainly had a wide choice in my youth, but none could be loved as I loved you. And all my long life I never met another, charming and accomplished as he might be, who measured up to you.

Our old cat, now fifteen, keeps me company in the house, and often Rory does, too. I am the last survivor among relatives of our generation, there is no one left to visit and stay over. Occasionally one or another from the next generations does so, but they are few and very busy. And I am not an energetic hostess. I get so tired, honey— a little physical activity goes a long way. With help I keep the house and garden decent and enjoy that.

No fatal illness in sight, can't be sure whether I'm glad or sorry. Maybe I still have time to clear away the masses of your papers in the many files, along with other memorabilia. In these nearly ten years I haven't been able to muster the energy to do that. In the beginning, when I tried, I found myself weeping and could not go on; I still can't. I'm ashamed; it's on my conscience, but I fear the children will have to do it all. I'd expected the cancer would metastasize again—or that the continued smoking would bring on the proverbial lung cancer. Everybody's hoping for that, I guess, to vindicate all the antismoking propaganda. Oh, sweetie, only you could be amused by that statement! Everybody worships the great god Health these days—and looks for habits, diets, and medical care that will keep them living forever, no matter how rotten life is. Nirvana is not to be reached that way! I can't reach it either. I still live in purgatory, but adaptation has helped me find comfortable corners where I can escape most of the unendurable pain I suffered in the beginning. I have found them through the rules of living I learned from you.

See you in the here, the hereafter, and the everywhere, my own true love—

Mimi